WINNER!

Paul Kropp

HIP-JR.

HIP Junior
Copyright © 2008 by Paul Kropp

LIBRARY AND ARCHIVES CANADA CATALOGUING IN PUBLICATION

Kropp, Paul, 1948–
    Winner! / Paul Kropp

(HIP jr)
ISBN 978-1-897039-31-1

    I. Title. II. Series.

PS8571.R772W565 2008   jC813'.54   C2008-902048-0

General editor: Paul Kropp
Text design and typesetting: Laura Brady
Illustrations drawn by: Catherine Doherty
Cover design: Robert Corrigan

    2 3 4 5 6 7   17 16 15 14 13 12

Printed and bound in Canada

Suppose your mom just won a lottery.
You'd be able to buy lots of great stuff,
and move to a cool house, and live the life
you always dreamed. Right?

Well, think again.

CHAPTER 1

We Won!

My mom was feeling good. And that was even before her big lottery win.

"I'm feeling happy," she said. She was making some dinner on the hot plate. It was beans and hot dogs . . . again. "I'm feeling lucky."

"Oh great," I groaned.

"Things are looking up," she went on. She was singing to herself. It was some old '80s rock music.

"Does that mean I can get my allowance?" I asked.

My mom stared at me. "Soon, Ryan. We're just a little short this week. But I'm good for it. Just trust me."

"Yeah, yeah," I groaned.

"And don't be such a downer. You're too young to be a downer."

My mom uses lots of old words like that. *A downer*. Then again, my mom is pretty old herself – thirty. I can't imagine being thirty. Even worse, I can't imagine being thirty and living in a motel. But as my mom says, you've got to look on the bright side.

Me? I'm eleven and I prefer the dark side. Give me some weird comics, that's all I ask.

"Dinner's on the table," Mom said.

"Oh joy," I replied.

"What's that?" Mom asked.

"I said, *Oh boy*. I'm really hungry."

In front of me was a plate of beans with two mini hot dogs. It looked kind of cool, with the hot dogs like eyeballs and the beans like hair. Then I gave it a smile with mustard. But the food didn't

have much taste. Canned food is like that.

We eat a lot of canned food because we don't have a real kitchen. In a motel room, you get a kitchenette. That's a too-small kitchen. There's a tiny fridge, a tiny sink, and a hot plate. That's why most of our meals come from cans.

We moved into the motel last year. My mom lost the job she had, and the money kind of disappeared. So did our old house. My mom got a new job cleaning rooms at the motel. Part of her pay is a free room and a free cell phone. So here we are, living in a motel. One room. One bed for my mom. One pull-out couch for me. And a kitchenette.

"You've got to look on the bright side," my mom said.

"Right," I told her.

"There are people starving out there."

"Right."

"But we have food and a good roof over our heads."

"A motel roof," I pointed out.

"Ryan, you are such a downer."

*   *   *

Later, I was sitting out on the porch while my mom watched TV. The porch is a little walkway in front of all the units. Each porch had two fold-up chairs so people could sit out. Since it had been pretty nice all May, I sat out a lot.

For me, sitting out meant quiet. Inside our room,

mom was shouting. She always shouted when she watched *Wheel of Fortune*. She shouted out the answers to all the questions. Sometimes, she was right. Sometimes she'd yell at the people on the TV. "C'mon you dummy. Ask for a D!" Sometimes she'd be wrong. Then she'd say, "Well, how about that?"

But she was always noisy. I think my mom was born noisy. And I was born quiet. Go figure.

I sat outside to use the cell phone. I was talking to my buddy Josh. We had to do a project for school. Our project was all about worms. Josh had a computer, so he had lots of facts about them. I had two books from school. Together, I thought that would be enough.

Anyhow, Josh said we should catch some worms. And I said I don't like worms. Then he said we should catch them and cut them up. He said we could draw the worm pieces for part of our project. And I said, you must be nuts. I hate worms!

So we were talking about worms. And my

mom was screaming.

"Ask for an E," Mom shouted.

Then, a bit later. "To be or not to be!!"

Josh asked me who was screaming. I told him it was my mom. I said she was a big *Wheel of Fortune* fan. Josh said, "I guess so."

Then it got very quiet inside. I guess *Wheel of Fortune* was over. It got a little noisy outside, with me on the phone.

"No real worms," I begged. "Pictures are okay, but not real worms!"

"Do you want an A?" Josh asked.

"Yeah, but not by cutting up a worm," I told him. "Let's set up a worm farm. Let's teach a worm to do tricks."

Josh thought I was an idiot. "A worm is not a dog. You can't teach a worm anything. It doesn't have a brain . . . "

He kept talking, but I didn't hear the rest. Inside our room, my mom let out a scream – an enormous scream. It wasn't a *Wheel of Fortune* scream. And it wasn't a "stubbed my toe" scream.

It was something I had never heard before – a scream of joy.

"I WON!" my mom screamed again. Then she repeated over and over again, "I WON! I WON! I WON!"

"Josh, I think I've got a problem here," I told my friend.

"Sounds like good news to me," he said.

My mom came rushing out the door. She was holding a lottery ticket in her hand. The look on her face was wild, almost crazy.

"We won, Ryan. We won! We won the 24/7 Lotto!"

I put the phone down and looked up. "Are you sure?"

Mom could hardly get her breath to speak. "I checked the number twice. It's right here, in my hand. The winning ticket!"

"So how much is it worth?" My mom got little wins all the time. Twenty bucks, fifty bucks, but never as much as she spends on lottery tickets.

"You won't believe it," Mom replied. Now she

was teasing me.

"A thousand dollars?"

"More."

"Twenty thousand?"

"More."

"A hundred thousand?"

Mom looked at me. Her blue eyes looked right into mine. She seemed to be putting the words together in her mind.

"You ready for it?" she asked.

I nodded. "So tell me."

Then my mom screamed again. "ONE POINT TWO MILLION DOLLARS!"

I gulped. The doors to some of the other units swung open. And there was a scream on our cell phone from Josh.

"Ryan," I heard through the phone, "you're rich!"

CHAPTER 2

Keeping It Quiet

I didn't believe my mother. Right away, I went in and checked the number. The ticket matched the jackpot number on TV. So I told mom to hide the ticket under the bed.

Then we both walked down to the corner store. They had the same jackpot number. My mom kept bouncing up and down. I thought she'd have to tell the man at the store or she'd explode right there. "Shhh!" I whispered. "No one has to know."

"But we won!" she whispered, grabbing my arm. "We're rich!"

"Just keep quiet," I told her. "As soon as people find out, they'll be all over us."

"So?" Mom asked.

"So . . . they'll all be asking for handouts. Do you want to *give* all the money away?"

"Well, some of it," Mom said. "Now we can afford to be good to our friends."

"Just be careful," I told her. "Don't tell your friends. Don't tell anybody until the money is in the bank. You've got to make a plan, Mom."

Mom just looked at me. "Ryan, how'd you get to be such a downer?"

Just for the record, I am not a downer. But I am careful. If you grew up like I did, you'd be careful too. My mom, if she ever got money, just blew it. There were parties and cars that didn't work. There were "sure thing" bets that didn't pan out. And then there were boyfriends. My mom has bad luck picking boyfriends. My own dad is in jail and the other boyfriends aren't much better. Mom will lend money to a boyfriend and never see him – or the money – again.

That's why I keep *my* money hidden. I don't tell Mom where I keep it, and I don't tell her how much I've got. If I did, it would be gone in a flash.

So I'm careful. And I knew *we* had to be careful. One point two million dollars is a lot of cash. But a lot of cash can go fast if you don't keep an eye on it.

On the way back to the motel, Mom promised to be quiet. And I didn't tell a soul. We had to let all this settle. We had to make some kind of plan for the money.

But when I got to school the next day, the news was all over.

"Hey, it's Ryan the rich kid," shouted the first guy I saw.

"Ryan, what you gonna buy?" shouted another. "A new car? A BMW? A Porsche?"

"Ryan," whispered a girl named Tracy. "I always thought you were a geek. But now – well, I can see how cool you really are. You want to come over to my house?"

"Hey, Ryan," said Bruce the Bully. "It used to be fifty cents not to get beat up. Remember? But for you, man, it's five bucks. Starting now."

Even the teachers had found out. "Ryan," said Mrs. Morton, "I'm so happy for you and your family. By the way, we're fundraising for the school trip. Do you think I could call your mom?"

How did they all find out? I only had to think for a second. Then the answer was clear. I could see it written on his face.

Josh.

"You told," I said.

"I had to," Josh admitted. "My mom heard me on the phone. She wanted to know who was rich. So then I had to explain, and she called her friends. So I called a couple of people. And then . . . it got out of hand." He looked kind of embarrassed. "You didn't say it was a secret."

"But I didn't say to blab it all over."

"Sorry," Josh replied. "But won't it be fun to spend the money. Me, I'd buy the new Xbox first, then the Wii. But if you've got over a million dollars – "

I cut him off. "How'd you know it was over a million?"

"I looked it up on the Internet. And the jackpot number was in the paper. When you go to pick up the money, *you'll* be in the paper.

"Oh joy," I muttered.

"What was that?" he asked.

"I said, oh boy. That's just what I want – to be famous for winning a lottery. It's not my money,

Josh. It's my mom's. And she has to figure out something smart to do with it."

"Your mom? Smart?" Josh raised his eyebrows. "Ryan, you've got a problem."

When I got home, my problem was waiting in the motel parking lot.

"Ryan, look," my mom said. "We've got a car." She pointed at a Jeep in front of our unit. The Jeep might have been cool – and most Jeeps are cool – but this one was pink.

"A pink Jeep?" I said.

"And I got such a good deal," she told me. "Less than $50,000. And I don't have to pay until we pick up the money."

"You spent fifty thousand bucks for a pink Jeep," I muttered.

"Oh, it's so much fun," my mom went on. "The car was right on the lot. And the salesman was so nice."

"I can just bet."

"Isn't it great?" my mom beamed. "And we're just getting started!"

"Oh joy," I muttered, for the second time that day.

"What was that?" Mom asked.

"I said, oh boy, let's go for a ride."

So we drove around town in the new Jeep. And it really was cool. I mean, we hadn't had a car for two years, so *any* car would be cool. But this new Jeep was *way* cool. It had everything! Even GPS so we couldn't get lost.

If only it wasn't pink.

When we got back, the cell phone was ringing. There were 14 messages left while we were gone. My mom said the phone had been going crazy all day.

"Everybody in town knows," she told me.

"Yeah," I groaned. "Everybody."

"So I called Uncle Fred," my mom said. "Like you said – we need a plan. Uncle Fred is really smart, and he said he'd help."

I remembered my Uncle Fred. He used to be married to mom's sister. Uncle Fred bought and sold houses. He drove flashy cars. And he smoked cigars. I'm not sure if Uncle Fred would be my first pick for help in all this, but my mom did the picking.

"He's got some ideas already," Mom said.

"Oh joy," I told her.

"What's that?" Mom asked.

"Oh boy," I lied for the third time. "I'm sure we can trust Uncle Fred."

CHAPTER 3

Trust Me

We waited two weeks to pick up the money. In those two weeks, my mom bought a lot of stuff. I began a list:

Pink Jeep $50,000

HDTV   7,000

Sound system   7,000

Cameras 3,000

Computers   5,000

New clothes   ?????

Party   3,000

So I figure she spent about $75,000 in two weeks. That didn't count the money she promised to friends. It seems that all mom's friends had a hard luck story. Mom was a sucker for hard luck stories. But mom didn't have any real money to give away . . . yet.

So I figured her $1.2 million was getting down to $1.1 million. And we still hadn't picked up the money yet. First, we had to wait for Uncle Fred to get a day free. He was coming along just in case there was trouble.

So when the big day came, Uncle Fred drove us in the pink Jeep. He took us to the Lotto office on Dundas Street. There was a big window for people who won more than $25,000. I mean you don't get that kind of payout at the corner store.

We lined up while other people picked up their prizes. One guy got fifty thousand, and he was really happy. One lady did a happy dance when she got her money.

Then my mom showed her ticket. The jackpot: one point two million dollars.

Suddenly, it was show time. They took us to a special room. There was a lot of paperwork to do. Then the pictures began.

The lottery people had a big cheque, the size of a blackboard. It wasn't real, but it was good for the pictures. They took one picture of my mom with the cheque, then me and my mom. Then Uncle Fred asked to be in a picture, so he got in one too. We were all smiling, even me. It's not every day you pick up over a million bucks.

23

On the drive home, Uncle Fred talked to Mom about a plan.

"You've got to get a house," he told my mom. "It's a good investment."

"Right," she said.

"And a business. You need to buy a business. For investment."

"Right," Mom said.

"So what kind of business? You want to run a store? How about a little photo shop? Or maybe a restaurant. You can cook, can't you?"

"Oh, sure," Mom said.

I kept thinking about canned beans and hot dogs.

"How about a comic book store?" I said.

"Quiet, kid," Uncle Fred told me. "Your mom and I are trying to make a plan here."

I guess a comic book store didn't fit in with Uncle Fred's plan. But wouldn't it have been cool?

"I was kind of thinking," Mom went on, "about the motel. I really like the place, and maybe we could buy it."

"A motel!" said Uncle Fred. "You've got over a million dollars, and you want to buy a motel."

"It's just an idea," Mom told him. But when my mom gets an idea . . . watch out!

So the two of them talked about the motel. What's a motel worth? How much money do you make? Well, neither of them knew. But Uncle Fred would find out.

We got back to the motel in about two hours. Uncle Fred let us out and went to park the Jeep. Mom and I headed for our room. My mom was beaming, holding on to her purse with all her might. I kept looking for crooks who might try to steal the money order.

But there were no crooks. Only a bald guy about my mom's age. He seemed to be hanging around, waiting. It turned out that he was waiting for us.

"Shelley," he said to my mother. "Don't you know me?" The guy stood with his hands stretched out, his face grinning.

"Uh, no," Mom said. "Or . . . uh, maybe. You're . . .

25

uh . . ."

"It's me, Jeff," the guy said, still grinning. "Your ex-husband!"

"But Jeff had long hair," Mom said. "And you're bald."

"Well, it's been a few years," the man said. "And prison life ain't easy."

My mom still gave him a funny look. "Jeff was thin and you're kind of fat."

"Prison food does that to a guy," the man said. "But it's me, the same old Jeff. Remember that trip we took to Texas? Remember how you cooked hot dogs and beans all the time."

"Uh, yeah, I guess so," Mom replied.

"Well, I'm back. Just came by to see you and my little guy, Ryan," he said. Then the guy looked right at me. "Come here and give your father a hug, son." He bent down and threw open his arms as if I were five years old.

I just stared at the guy. An ex-con thinks I'm going to give him a hug? He's got to be crazy.

"You don't remember me?" the guy asked.

I shook my head. How could I remember a guy I hadn't seen since I was two?

"Well, I think we need a little time to get to know each other," he said.

"Oh joy," I groaned.

"What was that?" the guy asked.

But this time I kept my mouth shut.

CHAPTER 4

Doubts

I had not seen my father for nine years. I was two when he went to jail. And my mom never told me where he went. For all I knew, my dad could be running a worm farm in the Yukon.

"You're really my father?" I asked. I stared at his face. He didn't look like me, not the least bit.

"Yup," the guy said. "Been locked up for nine years, I'm afraid. Just got out. Didn't your mom tell you?"

I looked at my mom.

"We never talked about that," she said coldly. "I told Ryan you were gone."

"Gone?"

"Like dead," my mom explained.

The bunch of us just stood there. The guy was still smiling. My mother looked like she had seen a worm. And Uncle Fred came walking up to us.

"So you're Jeff Malloy," my Uncle Fred said. "Back from the slammer."

Slammer. My mom wasn't the only person who liked old words.

"Yup," said the guy. "I heard about your good luck, so I just came by to say hello."

"And ask for money," Uncle Fred added.

The guy had a shocked face. "Me? Money? I wouldn't come back after nine years and ask for money."

"Then what do you want?" Fred asked.

"I want to get to know my son."

How touching, I thought. In a TV movie, the sucky music would start to play.

"And . . . ," my mom went on.

"And I could use a place to stay for a while, I guess."

My mom stared at him, then looked to my Uncle Fred. "I think we'll have to talk about that," she said.

My mom and Uncle Fred went off and talked. I stood with this guy. I kept looking at his face. Did he look like me? Would I look like that when I got old? Scary!

At last my mom came back and joined us.

"Okay, here's the deal," she said. "I think Unit

7 is empty at the motel. So I'll pay for the room for you. Until you get on your feet."

"Thank you," my father replied. "I really mean that."

"Sure you do," Mom said.

"No, I really do," my father said. "Once I'm set up, I'll be out of your hair."

"Right," my mom said. She was starting to sound like me.

All in all, it was quite a day. We picked up $1.2 million. And we found my long-lost father. A fortune . . . and a father, all in one day.

I really liked the fortune part. When you're rich, you stand a little taller. You sit up higher in the car. You look at things in store windows and say to yourself, I could buy that. So far, being rich really beat being poor.

I wasn't so sure about the father part. This old guy was a little strange. He kept picking at his teeth. And he scratched his head. And he didn't smell too good.

I didn't point any of these things out, of course.

I mean, he was my father. Maybe all those years in prison did things to you. Maybe prison is bad for your teeth.

But it did make me wonder.

"Are you sure he's your father?" Josh asked. We were talking on the phone kind of late.

"Sure I'm sure," I snapped back. "My mom said so."

"But is your mom sure?" he asked.

"Sure she's sure," I repeated. And that's hard to say fast.

"But maybe she made a mistake," Josh said. "It's been nine years. People change a lot in nine years."

"Yeah, true," I told him. "But that would be a big mistake. A *huge* mistake. I mean, my mom's not stupid."

Josh laughed. Sometimes I wonder why this guy is my friend.

But doubt is a tough thing. When you get some doubt in your brain, it won't just go away. You doubt something, then you try to believe it, but the doubt keeps coming back. It's like worms after a rain. They keep crawling from the ground. Yecch.

So the next day, I asked my dad a few questions. We were sitting on a pair of chairs outside his room, Unit 7. We were just talking. I wasn't checking, really. But I had this little bit of doubt about the dad thing.

"You remember when I was born?" I asked him.

"I'll never forget," he said. "You were such a cute baby."

"Was I?"

"Oh, yes. You were the cutest baby."

My mom always said I was a cute baby. But I guess all parents think their babies are cute, so what did it mean? Nothing. I kept on.

"And when I was little?" I asked.

"You were always getting into stuff," he replied.

"Like what?"

"Pots and pans. You were a very active baby, as I remember."

Okay, so that was true. I used to play with pots and pans. There are pictures to prove it. But still . . . there was this doubt.

"You remember my middle name?" I asked.

"Nah," he said. "I don't remember my own middle name. But give me a second. Did it start with a . . . a . . ."

"J," I told him.

"Yeah, Jason, or something like that," he said.

Well, there was some proof. My middle name is really Justin, but who cares? He came close. So I figured that my dad really was my dad. It was simple. The whole thing was simple.

Still, this big lottery win wasn't helping my life much. Bruce the Bully gives me trouble at school. All the other kids keep asking me for money. That girl Tracy is telling everyone that I'm her boyfriend. And now I have an ex-con father who picks his teeth.

And then, of course, it got worse.

"Ryan," my mom screamed, "come over here. I've got something big to tell you!"

CHAPTER 5

Big News

There were a bunch of people at the office of the motel. Up at the desk were my mom and Uncle Fred, with old Mr. and Mrs. Walters who owned the motel. There was an older lady who cleaned rooms, like my mom. There was the guy who fixed leaky toilets and broken windows. And there were a few other people I didn't know.

"Folks," began Mr. Walters, "we have something important to say here. This is really big news for all of us."

Then his wife picked up. "The Walters motel now has a new owner."

"And the new owner," said Mr. Walters, "is Shelley Malloy!"

All the rest of us began to clap, in a half-hearted kind of way. Mr. and Mrs. Walters were grinning. So were my mom and Uncle Fred. The rest of us looked kind of stunned.

"Thank you," my mom said. "I just want to say there will be no big changes for now. But next month, the new sign goes up. *Malloy's Motel!*"

Oh joy, I thought. But I kept my mouth shut.

There was more clapping, and then my mom brought out some wine. Another party. It seemed like we'd had a party every day since the big win. People would come for the party and stay to ask for money. Now that my mom could write cheques, the money was just pouring out. A couple of hundred here. A couple of thousand there.

"It makes them happy," my mom would say.

"So would a good comic book," I snapped back.

So the party began. There was lots of talk about how Mom would change the motel. A new office. New bathrooms. A big garden in the middle of the parking lot. A website: *www.malloysmotel.com.*

But I had one big question. How long would Mr. and Mrs. Walters stay on? They had the big owner's unit. The owner's unit had a *real* kitchen, a bedroom and a living room. It had twice as much room as our unit. I might even get my own bed.

"So, Mom," I asked her. "When do we move into the owner's unit?"

"We don't," she said.

"We don't? Why not?"

She gave me a big grin. "Because we're buying a house, Ryan. Uncle Fred has found us the perfect, perfect house."

"So it's nice?"

"Perfect, perfect," she repeated.

"When do we see it?"

"Soon, Ryan. Soon. I've only seen the house once myself." Then she giggled and went off to see a friend.

So many changes! Two weeks ago, we didn't own a thing. Okay, maybe our clothes, but that was about it. Now we owned a motel. And a house. And a pink Jeep. And all this *stuff*: a big TV, and a sound system, and computer games. We had gone from nothing to everything in two weeks. It was amazing.

The next day, we went to see the new house. Uncle Fred drove. My mom kept answering her cell phone. The paper had printed a photo of mom and Uncle Fred getting the big jackpot. Now her cell phone rang all the time.

"Oh, that sounds terrible," I heard my mom say. "Of course I can help . . ."

Uncle Fred shook his head. The phone rang again. That's when Uncle Fred picked up the phone, and then hung up. He didn't even listen.

"Come on, folks," he said. "Let's go see the new house."

Uncle Fred drove the Jeep. It felt like we were driving for hours, but I guess it was less than that. At last we reached a house on the edge of town. It was a pretty big house, maybe thirty years old. It looked plenty big enough for us.

"Here it is," Uncle Fred told us. "A great investment."

"And a lovely house," my mom said.

"Once the city comes out this far, this place will be worth twice what we're paying."

"How much is it?" I asked.

"Five hundred," he told me.

"Wow," I said, looking at the place again. "A

lot of house for five hundred dollars."

Uncle Fred just shook his head. "Five hundred *thousand*," he told me. "You're off by three zeroes, kid."

"Oh," I said. There was a funny lump in my throat. But what did I know about houses?

Still, it was a nice house. My mom and I went through the place room by room. There was a great big kitchen. There were three bedrooms and three bathrooms. There was a family room, a living room and a dining room. The place was huge! I mean, two of our motel units could fit into the *family* room. And then there was the pool, a real pool. It even had its own little house for changing your clothes.

"I love it," my mom said. We were walking back from the pool.

"The paperwork is all done," Uncle Fred told her. "I've kept the deed in my name, like I told you."

"In *your* name?" I asked.

Uncle Fred shot me a nasty look. "Yeah, for tax reasons."

"But it's our money," I told him. "It's a lot of our money."

Uncle Fred shot me a nastier look. "You gotta trust me, kid. I'm looking after your mother."

"Right," I said.

That's when my mom spoke up. "Fred, what about those cracks up there in the ceiling. Is that normal?"

"No problem," Fred told her. "It'll all be fixed up before you move in. No problem at all."

"Right," I said. I was repeating myself. But there was something about this that didn't feel right.

"In a month, say goodbye to that motel room," Fred told us. "You'll have a wonderful new life out here."

"Uh, right," I said for the third time.

A wonderful new life. Well, at least I wouldn't have to deal with Bruce the Bully and Tracy my girlfriend-not! But somehow this house didn't feel that good to me. Then I shook myself. Hey, what was my problem? Was my mother right all along? Was I becoming a *downer*?

CHAPTER 6

Friends and Family

After our pictures came out in the paper, things really went crazy. My mom's cell phone rang all the time. Old friends called. Relatives called. Strangers called.

Of course, all these people needed "just a little help."

My mom was a sucker for people who needed help. I think she'd given away almost $50,000 by the end of the first week. So then I had a talk with her.

"You've got to learn how to say no," I told her.

"No?" she replied.

"See, you've got it wrong. You can't have a question mark at the end. It has to be 'no, period.' Or sometimes a big NO!"

"But these people need help," Mom said. "They're friends. They're family."

I shook my head. "Help does not always mean money," I explained to her. "These guys just want a handout."

"But Aunt Rosie's cat . . . ," Mom whined.

"Is just a cat," I said. "You don't even know that Aunt Rosie has a cat."

"And my old friend Joanie," mom went on. "She just needed a little money to buy a house. That's all. It's a loan. She'll pay it back."

"Right," I said. "And some day pigs will fly."

My mom missed the point. She kept on wasting cash. I figured a lot of our money had been spent. We were down to maybe point two million. That is still $200,000, but the way mom was going, we'd be broke in a month.

Mom and I moved into the owner's unit when the Walters moved out. We wouldn't be there long, but it was nicer than our old room. My mom got rid of her old cell phone. She got a new one with a new number – an unlisted number.

Meanwhile, my father did nothing. As far as I could tell, he watched TV all day. Then he'd try to come over to our unit for dinner. Then he'd try to watch our big-screen TV. And then my mom would tell him to go back to his room.

"Was Dad always this lazy?" I asked Mom.

"Not in the old days," Mom told me. "But prison changes a man."

I had heard that line someplace before.

With the new cell phone, nobody knew how to reach us. The phone calls from friends and family stopped. My mom got back to *Wheel of Fortune*. She could get through a whole show with no rings.

But then friends and family got smart. They began to come over to the motel. A visit, they called it. A visit would start pretty friendly. Then some problem would come out. And then the call for a handout . . . sometimes with tears.

It would have been touching. Or funny. If my mom knew how to say no.

But one visit really changed things. My mom was watching her show – "Ask for a U, you idiot!" – and there was a knock on the door.

I went to see who was there. My mom didn't like visitors during *Wheel of Fortune*.

"Ah, Ryan," said the old lady at the door. "Could I see your mom?"

"She's kind of busy," I said. But that was when mom shouted out "It's Dancing with Wolves, Dancing with Wolves!"

"Okay, she's not that busy. And who are you?"

"Why, Ryan," said the woman, "you don't know your own grandma? I know I haven't been by to visit much, but still. It's me. Granny Malloy – your dad's mom!"

"Oh, of course," I said, smiling. "It's just . . . I don't have my glasses on."

Actually, I don't wear glasses. But that wasn't

the point. I hadn't seen Granny Malloy for nine years. Still, I had a hunch why she was knocking on our door. The same as all the others.

"Shelley, it's me," the old lady shouted.

"Just a minute," shouted my mom. "The show's almost over."

There was an awkward couple of minutes. Granny Malloy kept saying how tall I was. I felt like telling her that most kids don't shrink. But I didn't say that. Like my mom, I try to be nice.

At last, my mom came to the door. "Mrs. Malloy," Mom said. At least Mom knew who she was.

"Shelley, can I come in?" asked the old lady.

"Well, if you want to see Jeff, he's not here," my mom told her.

"Of course not," replied Granny Malloy. "I came to visit you, dear. I'm afraid Jeff still has another seven years to go."

My mom said what I thought. "Seven years to go?"

"If he's good," said Granny Malloy. "If he gets

in trouble again, it's ten more years."

"So he's not out of jail?" asked my mom.

"Of course not," said the old woman. "I visited him just last week. One of his buddies just got out, but not Jeff."

There was a long moment of silence. I could see my mom thinking. Her forehead gets all scrunched up when she thinks. At last my mom said, "Mrs. Malloy, I've got somebody for you to meet."

The three of us walked over to Unit 7. Mom pounded on the door. Inside, the TV got quiet. Then the door opened.

"Shelley," said the man who claimed to be my father. "I was just taking a nap."

"Right," replied my mom. "Do you know this lady?" she asked, pointing to Mrs. Malloy.

"Uh, well, I suppose."

"Do you *know* her?" Mom demanded.

"Uh, kind of."

My mom looked at Mrs. Malloy. "Granny, have you met this guy before?"

"Never in my life," she replied.

Then the shouting began. I had never heard my mom get that angry. "You cheat! You crook! You phony! You fraud! You imposter!" There were a few more words that I won't repeat here. And then Mom called the police on her new cell phone.

I wish the police would have been faster. As it was, my so-called father took off running. He was gone by the time the police car pulled up. My mom explained the whole thing to the cop. So now the guy can't even get near our motel.

I lost my father almost as fast as he showed up in my life. But I never did like the guy much. He didn't smell good and he picked his teeth.

And I did gain a grandmother. "Ryan, we have to get to know each other better," said Mrs. Malloy. "But first, I have to talk to your mom about this little problem of mine . . . "

CHAPTER 7

The New House

While all this was going on, my day-to-day life didn't change that much. Josh and I finished our worm project. Josh dug up some worms to fill a bottle. Then he cut up one worm and put the parts on a board. I took one worm and tried to teach it to do tricks.

All I can say is that worms are stupid. Three days I worked with that dumb worm and not one trick! Still, we got an a. That was one bit of good news.

I did figure out a way to deal with Bruce the Bully. I gave him IOUs instead of cash. In two weeks, Bruce had fifty bucks in IOUs. But I had a plan. By the time he was ready to collect, I'd be off at a new school.

Bye-bye Bruce and the IOUs. Bye-bye Tracy, who hangs around me at recess. Bye-bye Mrs. Morton who thinks I'm rich. And hello swimming pool!

Moving day was busy, busy. We didn't have much stuff to move, but there was still a lot to pack. My friend Josh came over to say goodbye.

"You know, Josh," I told him, "you're the only guy who never asked me for money."

"Really?" he said. "In that case, how about you lend me a hundred bucks. I'll pay you back. Honest, I will."

I stared at him.

"Just kidding," he said, and then we both laughed.

The moving truck pulled away. Mom and I followed in the pink Jeep. I waved goodbye to

Josh. I told him he could come swim in our pool next weekend.

But it didn't turn out that way.

We drove half an hour to the new house. The movers brought in all our stuff, but the place still looked empty. There was even an echo when we talked.

"Well, Ryan, we're here," Mom said.

"Our new home," I sighed. "Our new home with a swimming pool!"

My mom and I looked at each other. Then we spoke at the same time. "Let's go for a swim!"

We had to dig through boxes to find our bathing suits. Then we raced through the house and out to the pool. "Last person in is a rotten . . . ," I began, and then stopped.

The pool was covered in green scum.

And it smelled like pond slime.

"Oh dear," Mom sighed. "I guess the filter is broken."

"I guess," I said.

"We'll get the pool fixed next week," she told me. "And besides, it looks like it might rain."

"Right," I said. "No sense swimming in the rain."

So we raced back into the house. We plugged in our big HDTV to watch a movie. But the screen was just fuzz.

"I guess something happened to it in the move," Mom said.

"I guess," I said.

"We'll get it fixed next week."

We decided to make some dinner, but the gas was off. So we called for a pizza and sat down on the dining room floor.

"I've got to get a dining room set," my mom said.

"Good idea."

"And more living room furniture," she went on. "This place looks empty."

"Yeah. Kind of."

When the pizza guy showed up, it was raining outside. My mom and I were camped out on the floor. It was kind of fun. It was like real camping, but no tent and no bugs. We even made a campfire in the fireplace, but then smoke went all over.

"I'd better get that fireplace looked at," my mom said.

"Yeah," I agreed. We were both coughing.

"Still, it's a nice house," Mom said.

"Yeah, I guess," I replied. But Mom looked kind of upset, so I lied. "I mean, it's really great. Just a few things to get fixed."

"Wrinkles to be ironed out," Mom said.

"Bugs to be debugged."

Then we both started to laugh. We were still laughing when I felt a drop of water hit my head. This seemed strange. Water falling on my head – inside the house?

But then there was another drop. And another.

I looked at my mom. She was looking up, just the way I was. "Ryan, am I going crazy?"

We both looked up at the ceiling. We could see drops of water coming through the plaster. Even worse, we could see the plaster begin to bulge.

"Mom," I said, "I think we've got a problem."

"Ryan," she replied, "I think this problem could get worse."

The two of us got to our feet. I was going to start cleaning up the pizza camp-out when I heard a crack.

I looked up and the ceiling was starting to sag. Then I heard a second crack.

"Ryan, let's get out of here!" my mom yelled.

I heard the third crack while I was running. It was loud – crack! And then the whole ceiling came down. It sounded like a bomb going off.

"Oh joy," I muttered.

"What was that?" Mom asked.

"Oh boy, it's good that we weren't under the plaster."

"Right," my mom agreed. "But the TV sure is."

The two of us looked at the crushed TV. It would never show *Wheel of Fortune* again. It would never show anything ever again.

So we got into the pink Jeep and headed back to the motel. We checked ourselves into a room, and finished our pizza. Mom found *Wheel of Fortune* on cable, and she felt better.

I began to think about the new house. It would need a lot of fixing up. In fact, it was really a mistake to buy the place. But then I thought some more. Did we *really* buy the place? After all, it was Uncle Fred's name on the deed. For tax reasons. But if Uncle Fred owned the house, why was it our problem? Why wasn't it Uncle Fred's problem?

"Mom," I said just before I fell asleep, "I've got an idea."

CHAPTER 8

Home Again

My idea turned out to be a good one. The next day, my mom and I went to see a lawyer. I picked his name out of the phone book – Crooks. I figured that any guy with a name like Crooks couldn't be a crook. He just couldn't.

We told Mr. Crooks the whole story. He just kept shaking his head. Then Mom gave him the papers. He read them for ten minutes and then looked at me.

"Ryan, I think you're right. Your Uncle Fred has a leaky house on his hands."

"What about all the money we put in?" Mom asked.

"The deal hasn't closed yet," Mr. Crooks said. "You'll get it all back."

My mom sighed. I grinned. Maybe we weren't millionaires, but we weren't broke, either.

Mr. Crooks had lots of good ideas for my mom. The first one was to lock the money away.

Not from other people, but from her own good heart. He had us put a lot of money into the bank, locked away for a year. Nobody could touch it. Not even us.

Then he put $100,000 into a college fund for me. "Just in case you go to college," he said. "You can go in style."

And then he asked a big question. "Do you really want a house?"

"Well, sure," Mom said.

"But you have a big unit at the motel," Crooks said. "It's easier to run the motel if you live there. Why drive to work if you don't have to?"

Good point. So we put away enough money to buy a house, a small house, if we decide to do that.

Then my mom and I went shopping. My mom wanted some new furniture for our motel unit. And we needed a new HDTV, too. The old one didn't survive the leaky house.

So when we were settled, things were mostly good. We still got phone calls, but my mom learned to say no. "Sorry, the money is gone," she'd say. Gone to the bank, really. But gone.

My only problem was with Bruce the Bully. The IOUs were building up. And I wasn't going to a new school. So I went to my mom.

"I need a hundred dollars," I told her.

"For what?" she asked.

"A kind of school thing."

"What kind of school thing?"

"A project," I lied.

"Ryan . . . ," she said. It was that tone of voice. She saw right through me.

"Okay, not a project. I owe this kid some money."

"For what?"

"For not beating me up."

Now my mom got an angry look on her face. "That's bullying."

"Right."

"You can't give in to bullies."

"Right."

"No more than I can keep giving money to friends and family."

65

"Right," I said a third time. "But can I have the money, just this once?"

She shook her head. "Ryan, you just have to learn the way I did. No means no. You can't have a question mark at the end. It has to be 'no, period.' Or sometimes a big NO!"

I think I heard somebody else say that once.

I was going to beg some more, but the cell phone rang. My mom pushed the talk button.

"Hello," she said, "yes, this is Shelley Malloy. Yes, yes, I did put my name in. Would I like to be on *Wheel of Fortune?* Is that you, Mr. Sajak? Is that really you?"

I guess Mom's lucky streak isn't over yet.

The Crash

by PAUL KROPP

A school bus slides off a cliff in a snowstorm. The bus driver is out cold. One of the guys is badly hurt. Can Craig, Rory and Lerch find help in time?

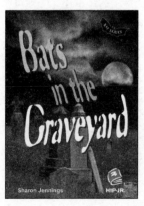

Bats in the Graveyard

by SHARON JENNINGS

Sam and Simon have to look after Simon's little sister on Halloween night. Soon the boys end up in a cemetery — spooked!

**P**aul Kropp is the author of more than fifty novels for young people. His work includes nine award-winning young adult novels, many high-interest novels, as well as books and stories for both adults and early readers.

Paul Kropp's best-known novels for young adults, *Moonkid and Liberty* and *Moonkid and Prometheus*, have been translated into many languages and have won awards around the world. His high-interest novels have sold nearly a million copies in Canada and the United States. For more information on Paul, visit his website at www.paulkropp.com.

For more information on HIP novels:

High Interest Publishing
www.hip-books.com